MW00880155

For Aunt Anne and all of the "Littles" she loves
—K.D.

To my lovely wife, Brandy, and our "Little," Maddox
—A.G.F.

Text copyright © 2017 by Kelly DiPucchio
Jacket art and interior illustrations copyright © 2017 by AG Ford

All rights reserved. Published in the United States by Doubleday, an imprint of Random House Children's Books,
a division of Penguin Random House LLC, New York.

Doubleday and the colophon are registered trademarks of Penguin Random House LLC.

Visit us on the Web! randomhousekids.com

Educators and librarians, for a variety of teaching tools, visit us at RHTeachersLibrarians.com

Library of Congress Cataloging-in-Publication Data
Names: DiPucchio, Kelly, author. | Ford, AG, illustrator.
Title: Littles : and how they grow / by Kelly DiPucchio ; illustrated by AG Ford.
Description: First edition. | New York : Doubleday, [2017] | Summary: A rhyming celebration of babies,
or Littles, who are cared for by loved ones in every way and grow big in the blink of an eye.
Identifiers: LCCN 2016021204 (print) | LCCN 2016051336 (ebook) |
ISBN 978-0-399-55526-8 (hc) | ISBN 978-0-399-55527-5 (glb) | ISBN 978-0-399-55528-2 (ebk)
Subjects: | CYAC: Stories in rhyme. | Babies—Fiction. | Family life—Fiction.
Classification: LCC PZ8.3.D5998 Lit 2017 (print) | LCC PZ8.3.D5998 (ebook) |
DDC [E]—dc23
MANUFACTURED IN CHINA
10 9 8 7 6 5 4 3 2 1
First Edition

Littles

And How They Grow

Kelly DiPucchio · illustrated by AG Ford

Doubleday Books for Young Readers

Littles are loved from the moment they're born.

They're swaddled,

and coddled,

and kissed every morn.

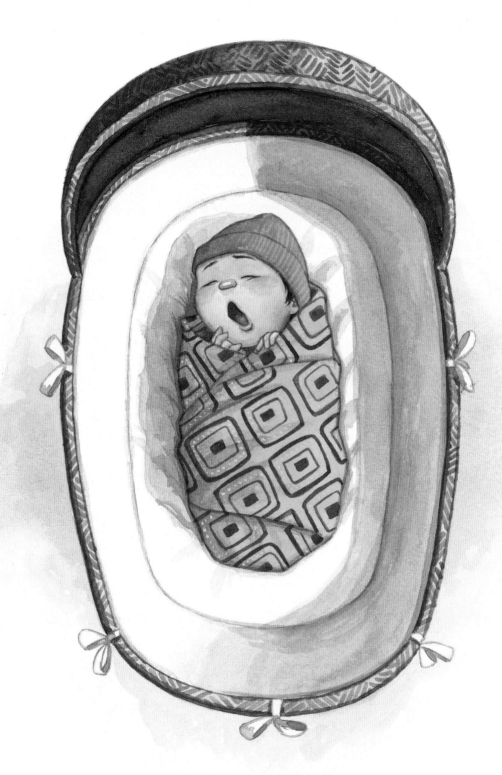

Littles are cuddled and cradled just right.

On bellies, with blankies,

in slings snuggly tight.

Littles are washed in warm, bubbly baths,

with duckies and daddies

that quack and who laugh.

Littles are dressed in snug sleepers and tees
and onesies that show off
their sweet dimpled knees.

Littles are fed on soft laps and in chairs.

They're nursed and they're spoon-fed

cooked carrots and pears.

Littles are soothed when they're sassy or scared,
through tantrums and new teeth

and toys that aren't shared.

Littles are cherished by kindhearted kin,

who sway and who play and make peekaboo grins.

Littles are read to in all kinds of places,

by all kinds of people with beaming, bright faces.

Littles are walked in wide meadows and malls,
in cities, on seashores,

down long moonlit halls.

Littles are sung to on quilts and in cars,

in rainstorms and rockers and under the stars.

Littles are busy!

Days will fly by . . .

. . . and littles grow BIG

in the blink of an eye.